ROYAL RESCUES

The Cuddly Seal

Paula Harrison

illustrated by Olivia Chin Mueller

WITHDRAWN

Feiwel and Friends · New York

For Jacob and Samuel

A Feiwel and Friends Book
An imprint of Macmillan Publishing Group, LLC
120 Broadway, New York, NY 10271

Our books may be purchased in bulk for promotional, educational, or business
use. Please contact your local bookseller or the Macmillan Corporate and
Premium Sales Department at (800) 221-7945 ext. 5442 or by email at
MacmillanSpecialMarkets@macmillan.com.

Library of Congress Cataloging-in-Publication Data is available.

ISBN 978-1-250-79113-9 (hardcover)
1 3 5 7 9 10 8 6 4 2

ISBN 978-1-250-25932-5 (trade paperback)
1 3 5 7 9 10 8 6 4 2

ISBN 978-1-250-25931-8 (e-book)

Book design by Nosy Crow and Cindy De la Cruz
Feiwel and Friends logo designed by Filomena Tuosto

First American edition, 2021.
First published in the UK by Nosy Crow
as *Princess of Pets: The Cuddly Seal* in 2020.

mackids.com

Chapter One
A Day by
the Sea

Bea skipped down the beach with a
picnic basket in one hand and a bucket
in the other. It was a perfect summer's
day, and seagulls were circling around
the fishing boats as they chugged across
the sparkling sea into the harbor. A
warm breeze swept across the bay, lifting
Bea's hair and making the waves dance.

"Come back, Bea!" yelled Natasha,

Bea's older sister. "We don't want to eat the picnic so close to the water. We'll get soaked when the tide comes in."

Bea dug her toes into the warm sand. She couldn't wait to go swimming with Keira, her best friend, who had joined them for the day. They had all set off from Ruby Palace with their buckets and shovels and swimming towels, accompanied by Nancy, one of the palace maids.

Bea was the middle one of the three royal children. Alfie, her little brother, had been bouncing around the palace with his fishing net since six o'clock that morning. Bea wasn't surprised that their dad, King George, had looked so relieved as he waved them off from the front steps. He'd glanced at Bea sternly just before they left. "Remember, Beatrice!

No bringing home stray dogs or cats or hamsters. In fact, don't pick up anything furry at all!"

Bea had made a face. Everyone knew she was animal-mad. She was always on the lookout for animals that needed her help, and she had already rescued a kitten and a puppy, as well as a tiny reindeer called Marshmallow and a pony named Sandy. Each time she rescued an animal the king would say, "Beatrice, the palace is no place for a pet!" But Bea knew in her heart that she would never be able to resist a creature in trouble.

"Hurry up, Bea!" Natasha shouted. "Alfie says he's hungry."

"All right—I'm coming!" Bea swung the basket as she walked back up the beach.

Natasha began laying out the picnic

blanket. Keira helped Bea to unpack all the rolls and cakes, and the big bottle of lemonade. "My mom and dad sent some food, too." She unzipped a large lunch bag. "There are samosas and pastries, and homemade chocolate-chip cookies."

Alfie made a dive for Keira's bag at once. Keira's parents ran the Sleepy Gull Café on the cliff top, and everyone knew their food was the best in the whole of Savara.

"Alfie, don't grab like that," scolded Natasha. "You're a prince, not a puppy."

Keira giggled. "It's all right! My mom and dad sent plenty."

"That's lucky with Alfie around," Bea joked, giving her little brother a nudge.

After finishing the picnic, Bea and Keira walked down to the shore. They were wearing bathing suits under their clothes, so they pulled off their shorts and T-shirts and jumped straight into the warm water. The sea made a gentle shooshing noise as it rolled onto the sand. Bea leapt over each wave, splashing water everywhere. Then the girls dived right in, pretending they were mermaids as they swam through the shallows.

"Nancy!" Bea called up the beach. "Can we go to Silver Rock Bay and look at the caves?"

Silver Rock Bay was a smaller cove just around the corner from the main beach. The sand there was a beautiful pale color, and there were exciting caves to explore. Bea had been allowed to play there before, as both she and Keira were strong swimmers and had gotten their grade three first-aid certificates.

The cove could only be reached at low tide when the water rolled back, leaving room to walk past the rocky headland.

"Yes, you can, Princess Bea," Nancy called back. "But please be sensible."

Bea and Keira put their shorts and T-shirts back on and walked around the rocky headland. The seagulls wheeled over their heads. Little tufts of yellow and orange flowers bloomed on the cliff face.

The girls rounded the corner into Silver Rock Bay. Pink-and-white shells were strewn across the gleaming sand. Rows of dark caves lined the back of the beach, and around the edge were the silvery rocks that gave the bay its name.

"Look at those shells!" cried Bea. "I've never seen so many pretty ones."

"They're lovely!" Keira picked up a

curly shell and held it to her ear. "I can hear the sea!"

Keira and Bea played in the waves for a while before exploring the largest cave at the back of the beach. It was dark and cool inside, and when they called loudly, it made a brilliant echo. The girls climbed over the rocks at the cave entrance, looking into the rock pools for little crabs and tiny fish.

"We'd better go back," Keira said after a while. "We don't want to get trapped in the bay once the tide comes in."

They walked back to the shore. The breeze had grown stronger, and the sea was dotted with thousands of tiny white-flecked waves.

Bea shaded her eyes and stared at the far end of the beach. "What's that funny shape? Do you think someone left their picnic bag behind?" She pointed to a little white blob on the rocks.

Keira frowned. "I think it moved!"

Bea started running, calling over her shoulder, "I'm going to see!" She sped across the sand, slowing down as she drew closer to the shape. Keira ran after her.

The shape was curved and covered with downy-white fur as soft as a cloud. Bea's stomach swooped with excitement. "It's a little seal pup! But what's it doing here all alone?"

"My dad says baby seals feed on their mother's milk," Keira told her. "But after a few weeks the mother goes back out to sea. Then the pup follows her later."

"But seal families usually gather

together on the same beach, so why is this pup the only one here?" Bea knelt down on the sand, and the seal pup turned its big black eyes to her. Lifting its whiskery nose, it gave a tiny little yelp.

"Oh, poor thing!" Keira crouched beside Bea. "Do you think it's waiting for its mother to come back?"

"I guess so." Bea touched the pup's snow-white fur. He was the softest, most beautiful animal she'd ever seen.

"Your dad told you not to even pick up anything furry," Keira reminded her.

"I know." Bea sighed. "But this baby seal is much too small to be here by himself. I wish I knew how to help."

Just then, Nancy appeared around the rocky headland leading back to the main beach. Waving her arms, she shouted, "Princess Bea! Keira! The tide's coming in and Prince Alfie's banged his knee."

"We'd better go!" Bea made a face. "Bye, little seal pup."

The baby seal pulled himself forward with his flippers. Sliding into a shallow rock pool, he lay there splashing and yelping happily. The girls laughed.

Then, reluctantly, they hurried across the beach and around the headland.

Bea looked back as she turned the corner. She could just make out the furry white shape beside the rocks. She wished more than anything that she didn't have to leave the baby seal pup all alone.

Chapter Two
HMS
Bouncing Barnacle

The following morning, King George decided to take Bea, Natasha, and Alfie on a boat trip.

They walked down to the harbor and climbed aboard the royal boat, the HMS *Bouncing Barnacle*. Bea fizzed with excitement as she walked down the gangplank to the wooden deck.

"Where are we going today, Dad?" asked Natasha.

King George, who was dressed in his navy sailing suit and cap, untied the mooring rope. "We're going to visit somewhere very special called Nala Island."

"Ooh, an island!" Alfie's eyes lit up. "Is it special because there's buried treasure? We could pretend we're on a pirate ship and we've returned to the island to get our gold."

"No, there's no treasure, but there's lots of wildlife at this time of year and that's why it's such an extraordinary place." King George didn't notice Alfie's disappointed pout. He pulled in the gangplank, stowing it safely on the deck. "Let's raise the anchor and go!"

Mrs. Stickler, the palace housekeeper, left the picnic basket in the cabin before handing around orange life jackets. Then the *Bouncing Barnacle* glided smoothly out of Savara Harbor. The king turned the wheel, guiding the boat toward a small rocky shape in the distance.

The *Bouncing Barnacle* had a powerful engine, and sometimes Bea felt as though they were flying across the water. Natasha liked to sit inside at the small cabin table, but Bea preferred perching at the front to watch the prow of the boat cutting through the water and throwing up sparkling rainbow spray.

The *Bouncing Barnacle* slowed down as they drew closer to Nala Island. Bea leaned over the prow to gaze at the clear turquoise water. Shoals of little silver fish swam away from the approaching ship, and the fronds of scarlet sea anemones swayed gently.

A wide sandy beach came into view, with a tall cliff behind it dotted with nesting seabirds. Bea stared at a cluster of gray and white shapes lying on the sand. "Look!" she burst out. "Seals with their pups!"

King George smiled. "At this time of year the Nala beaches are full of seals and their young. It's quiet here, and there are plenty of fish to eat when they return to the sea."

Their dad continued explaining how the seals made their home on Nala Island, but Bea wasn't listening. She twisted around, looking back toward Savara. Next to the main beach was Silver Rock Bay, where she'd found the seal pup the day before. She wondered whether the baby seal was all right and if his mother had come back to find him.

King George switched off the engine, and they glided quietly toward the island until their dad lowered the anchor. "We mustn't disturb the young seals and their mothers," he explained. "So we won't take the boat any closer, but you can swim right here if you like!"

Alfie gave a cheer. Then he pulled off his life jacket and shorts, leaving just his swimming trunks, and jumped in. Natasha took off her life jacket and climbed sedately down the ladder.

"Now listen, Beatrice," the king added. "Don't get any ideas about bringing a seal back to the palace."

"No, Dad!" Bea was still thinking of the seal pup as she followed Natasha down the ladder. She had really wanted to take him home, but perhaps his mother had come back for him. She dipped her toes into the warm water before sliding in. At once a gray whiskery face popped up close by. The seal watched Bea curiously for a moment before diving below the water.

"Look at me!" Alfie called. "I'm swimming with the seals."

"Shh, Alfie!" Natasha said, paddling up to her brother. "We're not meant to disturb the ones on the beach, remember?"

Bea loved the way the seals twisted

and turned, pulling themselves along
with their powerful flippers. When they
bobbed up to the surface, the sunlight
gleamed on their silky coats. The beach
beyond was full of furry white seal pups.
Bea smiled as she listened to their yelps
and the deeper barking replies of the
mother seals.

"Come back now, children. It's lunchtime," called Mrs. Stickler sharply.

Bea swam reluctantly back to the boat, climbed up the ladder onto the deck, and wrapped a towel around herself. A growling engine noise started up just as she took a cheese-and-ham roll from the picnic basket.

"What on earth is that?" King George looked up in surprise. "Boats shouldn't be fishing this close to the island."

Bea ran to the bow and saw a small red boat chugging into view. It sailed right up to the nearby beach, and two men jumped out carrying fishing rods. The larger seals began barking loudly, and some of the seal pups wriggled away in alarm.

"They're scaring the pups!" cried Bea. "They shouldn't have landed there

at all." King George frowned. "The rule
is: keep away from mother seals with
their young because they shouldn't be
disturbed. Stay here, children. I shall go
and speak to them." He unloaded the
inflatable dinghy and set off for the
shore.

"Honestly! I thought everyone knew
you shouldn't disturb the wildlife here,"
said Natasha. "It's an important nature
reserve. Pass the cookies please, Bea."

"Maybe Dad's going to arrest them!"
said Alfie, his eyes big and round.

"That's enough silliness," said Mrs.
Stickler.

King George spoke to the men on
the shore, and they set off in their boat
again. When the king returned to the
Bouncing Barnacle, everyone continued
enjoying their lunch, except for Bea,

who studied the beach worriedly. Each of the baby seals had returned to their mother except for a tiny one that sat forlornly by the water's edge. Was he lost? What would happen when the tide came in if he wasn't ready to swim?

Bea suddenly wondered if the same thing had happened to the seal pup she'd found the day before. Maybe he wasn't meant to be in Silver Rock Bay at all. Maybe he'd been swept away from his real home. "Dad, can I talk to you about something?" she asked.

King George was pouring himself a cup of tea from a flask. "I really must arrange for some signs to go on that island," he said to Mrs. Stickler. "Then everyone will understand that landing on those beaches is not allowed."

"That's a good idea, sire," Mrs.

Stickler replied. "People are very thoughtless at times."

"Dad?" Bea tried again. "I saw something yesterday and I think you should know—"

"Just a minute, Beatrice. I'm talking to Mrs. Stickler," her dad said. "Now, what do you think the signs should say?"

Bea huffed a little and leaned against the side. There was no point trying to get her dad's attention when he was busy thinking about something else.

The seal pup beside the water's edge moved back up the beach again. Bea watched in relief as the little pup stopped beside a large gray seal and cuddled into her side.

King George started the engine and steered the *Bouncing Barnacle* back

toward the mainland. Bea stared over
at Silver Rock Bay as they crossed the
waves. The bay was easy to make out,
with its row of dark caves at the bottom
of the cliff, but she couldn't see the baby
seal anymore. Was he still there, or had
he found the strength to swim away? He
could be camouflaged against the silvery
white rocks.

Bea held the side of the boat tightly
as they bounced through the waves. She
needed to know that the seal pup was all
right. As soon as they landed, she would
go to find out.

Chapter Three

A Fish
or Three

Bea wanted to hurry over to Silver
Rock Bay the moment they drew up to
the harborside, but Mrs. Stickler wouldn't
let her go. She seemed to have an extra
sense for when Bea was about to dash
off somewhere.

"Please take this, Princess Beatrice."
She handed Bea the picnic basket. "I
need some help carrying everything
back to the palace."

Bea tried not to frown as she took the basket handle. "Yes, Mrs. Stickler."

The harbor was full of people washing the decks of their boats and mending their sails. The king waved to people cheerily as he went by. A row of stalls by the harbor wall were selling freshly caught fish. Soon the fishing boats would return to the sea to make their catches for the next day.

Bea trudged up the hill behind Natasha and Mrs. Stickler. She wished she could escape to the beach. If she didn't go soon, the tide would come in and cut off Silver Rock Bay. Then it would be too late to check on the seal pup.

When they reached the palace, she left the picnic basket in the royal kitchen and hurried back to the front door, hoping for a chance to slip away.

"Princess Beatrice, I expect you need

a bath after all that swimming in the sea." Mrs. Stickler stood at the palace entrance, blocking the way.

"Alfie should go first!" Bea said quickly.

"All right, then." The housekeeper marched over to the stairs, calling, "Prince Alfred! Where are you?"

As soon as Mrs. Stickler disappeared upstairs, Bea dashed to the back door. She ran through the palace garden and raced all the way down the hill to Savara, stopping to catch her breath as she reached the seafront.

The beach was empty. A strong breeze blew in from the sea, sending a piece of seaweed dancing across the sand. Bea took off her sandals and raced to the water's edge. Splashing through the rock pools, she hurried around the headland into Silver Rock Bay.

Far away across the sand, she spotted
a little white shape lying between two
rocks. The seal pup hadn't moved very
far since the day before, and there was
no sign of his mother.

Bea ran to him and knelt down
on the sand, gently stroking his fluffy
white coat. The seal lifted his head a
little and gave a tiny yelp. His eyes
looked duller than before, and Bea
frowned. "You poor thing! I'm sure
it's not right that you're here all
alone."

"Bea!" A hand tapped Bea's shoulder and she jumped.

"Keira!" Bea scrambled up. "I didn't know you were going to be here."

Keira grinned. "I wanted to check that the seal pup was all right. We must have had the same idea!"

Bea nodded. "We went out on the boat this morning, and I couldn't stop thinking about him." She told Keira about the trip to Nala Island and the men with the red boat who had disturbed the baby seals on the beach. "So maybe something like that happened to our seal, too. Maybe he's not really meant to be here."

"That makes sense!" Keira pushed her ponytail over her shoulder. "But why isn't his mother looking for him? He must need her milk."

Bea climbed onto the rocks and shaded her eyes as she looked out to sea. "I don't know, but I can't see any seals nearby."

Keira scrambled up beside her, and together they gazed at the water. Bea kept hoping that a gray seal's head would pop up above the surface, but nothing happened.

"Maybe the little pup will go back to the sea to find his family," suggested Keira doubtfully.

"I don't know how he can when he looks so weak." Bea rubbed her forehead. "We have to help him. If his mother hasn't come back, we'll have to bring him some fish to eat."

"That's a great idea!" Keira's eyes lit up. "We have lots of fish back at the café."

"Let's go to the harbor—it's even closer." Bea jumped down from the rocks and took some coins from her pocket. "I still have some pocket money I can spend."

The girls stroked the seal pup before running back along the beach. They stopped, panting, when they reached the harbor. The fish sellers were starting to pack up their stalls. Sailors were shaking out their nets and sweeping the decks of their boats.

"What kind of fish do seals like?" Bea whispered to Keira.

"I don't know!" Keira made a face. "Maybe some tuna . . . or cod or sardines?"

"Let's get all of them." Bea marched over to a fair-haired woman sitting behind the nearest stall. "Excuse me!

Could we buy some tuna, cod, and sardines, please?"

"Of course!" The woman smiled and put some white fish on her weighing scales. "How much would you like of each?"

"Er, I'm not sure." Bea frowned. "Just a little bit, I suppose. This is how much money I have." She showed the woman a handful of coins.

The fish seller looked surprised. "All right then! I'll parcel them up for you." She weighed the three pieces of fish and wrapped them up in paper.

"Thank you!" said Bea, taking the parcels of fish. The girls hurried along the harborside, nearly bumping into Douglas, a fisherman with a white beard and wrinkled face who Bea knew very well. Douglas drove the royal boat from

time to time when the king wanted
some help. He had taken the royal
family on many trips along the coast.

"Hello, Princess Bea." Douglas smiled.
"You seem in an awful hurry."

"We're helping a little seal pup. He's
ever so small and cute." Bea smiled back.
"Are you going out to sea to catch more
fish soon?"

"Not today. There's a storm coming."
The fisherman nodded at the sky, where
dark clouds were thickening. "No point
in risking the boat when the sea is
rough."

Bea and Keira exchanged worried
looks. A gust of wind blew across the
harbor, making the ships' sails flutter.

"We should hurry," Bea said to Keira.
"The tide gets higher when there's a
storm. Bye, Douglas! See you soon."

The girls rushed down the harbor steps and along the shore. The wind whipped up little whirlpools of sand on the empty beach. Bea ran faster, the fish parcels tucked under her arm. She and Keira raced around the headland as a cluster of storm clouds swarmed across the gray sky.

Chapter Four

Danger on the Shore

Bea spotted the enormous gulls as soon as she and Keira reached Silver Rock Bay. There were three of them strutting along the sand and squawking to each other. Bea glanced at the smaller seabirds nesting on the cliffs. These gulls were bigger and meaner, with white bodies and black wings. They stalked toward the baby seal with a nasty look in their eyes.

"The seal pup!" cried Keira, and she and Bea began to run.

One of the gulls hopped onto a rock beside the seal. Tilting its head, it leaned toward the pup.

"Shoo!" Bea yelled, waving her arms frantically.

"Hey!" Keira joined in, flapping her arms, too. "Get away from that seal."

The three gulls flew into the air before landing a little way off. They kept on strutting up and down the sand, watching the girls with their beady yellow eyes.

Bea stopped beside the seal pup, her heart pounding. "Those horrible birds! I don't trust them at all."

"Let's try giving him the fish," Keira said breathlessly. "If he gets stronger, he'll be able to swim away into the sea."

Bea knelt down and unwrapped the first parcel. "Here you are. Are you hungry?" She held out the tuna, the smell of raw fish filling her nose.

The pup sniffed at the fish, his whiskers twitching. Bea waited hopefully for him to take a bite, but his head sank onto the sand again.

"Maybe he likes a different kind of fish." Keira unwrapped the next parcel and offered the pup the sardines.

This time the seal hardly lifted his head at all. When Bea put the parcel of cod beside him, he ignored that, too.

Bea laid all the fish aside. "What's wrong, little seal?" She rubbed his soft white fur. "Don't you want any fish?

You have to eat if you're going to get stronger."

"Maybe he's too young and he really needs milk," said Keira.

"We have to do something!" Bea glanced at the gulls prowling nearby. "As soon as we leave, those horrible birds will be back."

"We could move him into that big cave," Keira suggested. "I've never seen any gulls go in there."

Bea frowned. She wasn't sure if a dark cave would be scary for the seal pup, but they had to get him away from the huge seagulls. "At least if his mother comes back, she'll still be able to find him."

Keira pulled off her sweater. "Let's wrap him in this and carry him over."

They laid the sweater on the sand,

and after a lot of pushing and tugging,
they managed to slide the seal pup onto
it. The little animal opened his black eyes
wide and stared at the girls in surprise.

"It's all right! We're going to take care
of you." Bea lifted the seal into her arms,
smearing sand all over her T-shirt and
Keira's sweater.

The pup felt heavy, and Keira had to help by holding up his round tummy. He began to squirm as they carried him up the beach, wriggling his tail and flippers. His whiskers shook, and he twitched his nose as if he was about to sneeze.

Bea held the seal pup tight as he began to yelp. "Don't be scared! We're only taking you to the cave. You'll be safer there!"

"Let's lay him on that sandbank." Keira nodded at a ridge of sand at the back of the cave. "He'll be tucked out of the way, but he'll still be able to see the ocean."

Bea's arms began to ache, and her foot slipped a little on a wet rock.

"Bea, are you all right?" Keira dived forward, holding the seal under his tummy.

"Don't worry—I'm fine." Steadying herself, Bea carried the baby seal the last few steps, and removing Keira's sweater from around his tummy, she set him down gently on the sand.

Cool air drifted through the cave, and water dripped down the smooth walls. The baby seal wriggled and sniffed the air before laying his head on the sand as if he was tired from all the excitement.

Bea knelt down beside the seal pup. "I promise we'll come back to check on you tomorrow." She swallowed. Tomorrow seemed such a long way off.

What if the seal pup needed her before then?

Keira stroked the seal's head. "Look at his big dark eyes! I think he's the cutest thing I've ever seen."

The pup gave a long mew and twitched his whiskers.

Bea laughed. "I think he agrees with you! He's certainly the furriest creature I've ever met. I guess he needs all that fluff to keep out the cold sea wind."

"We should think of a name for him," Keira said suddenly. "How about Snowy because of his lovely snow-white fur?"

"Snowy suits him!" Bea grinned, but then her smile faded. "I know he's safer here, but I wish we didn't have to leave him!"

"I want to stay, too." Keira looked out the cave entrance. "But the tide's really coming in now, so we'd better go!"

Bea gave Snowy one last stroke before she and Keira hurried out of the cave. The sea poured into the bay, washing away their footprints from the sand. The nasty-looking gulls croaked to each other and flapped away over the cliffs. The wind grew fiercer, turning the waves into mounds of white foam.

Keira and Bea raced round the headland just as the tide reached the rocks. Savara Beach was empty, with just a few sandcastles scattered across the shore.

"Everyone's gone home early," said Keira.

Bea glanced at the dark clouds marching across the sky. "I guess they didn't want to be caught in the storm. The sea looks rough already."

"At least Snowy will stay safe and dry in the cave." Keira shook the sand off her sweater and put it back on.

The wind surged across the seafront, shaking the palm trees. Bea said goodbye to Keira. Then she headed for home, struggling up the hill against the rising wind. She hoped the seal's mother would come back to find her pup. The little animal certainly needed someone to look after him.

Chapter Five
The Moonlit Cave

The sky grew darker, and the wind whistled around the palace all the way through dinner that evening. Bea tried not to worry about the seal pup as she ate her chicken pie and carrots. Luckily, no one had noticed she'd left Ruby Palace earlier that afternoon, though Mrs. Stickler had asked her sharply whether she'd had her bath yet.

Heavy rain was pouring down by the

time Bea got changed for bed. She put on her pawprint pajamas and sat on the windowsill, watching puddles growing on the palace drive and water dripping from the lemon trees in the orchard.

There were thumping footsteps outside the door, and Alfie burst in. "I'll never sleep if there's thunder and lightning. It's too exciting!"

Bea smiled. She didn't mind Alfie rushing in like a brother-shaped tornado. At least he was stopping her from worrying about the seal pup. "Maybe there won't be much thunder this time."

Natasha appeared in the doorway in her gold satin pajamas, her hair neatly brushed. "Mrs. Stickler says you should both be in bed—especially you, Alfie."

"We were just talking about how bad the storm might be," said Bea.

"The worst weather won't arrive till tomorrow morning," Natasha told them. "Mrs. S. looked up the weather forecast."

Bea's heart lifted. Maybe there would

be another chance to check on Snowy before the storm arrived.

"It's a good thing we had our day at the beach yesterday," Natasha went on. "Nancy says those caves you went in get flooded every time there's a storm. There'll be water everywhere!"

Bea stared at her sister. "You mean the ones in Silver Rock Bay? But the shoreline is a long way from the caves."

"I know, but that's what Nancy told me," Natasha insisted. "She remembers how deeply they flooded in the last storm. Come on, Alfie. It really is bedtime!"

Alfie followed Natasha, grumbling loudly.

Bea paced up and down her bedroom, her heart racing. She and Keira hadn't kept the baby seal safe after all. She pictured Snowy looking confused as the sea flooded into the cave, filling the rock pools and covering the sand. She had to rescue him before the water got that far! But it was dark outside ... and there was no chance of even reaching Silver Rock Bay until low tide.

She sank onto the windowsill again, frowning at the raindrops sliding down the glass. Natasha had said the storm wouldn't reach the shore till morning. Maybe she could leave the palace very early tomorrow and move the seal before the storm reached the cave.

Bea ran down to the palace kitchen and read the list of tide times pinned to the wall. The tide would be low by five o'clock. If she went then, she would reach the cove safely. Maybe she could fetch the seal and bring him back to the palace. Her dad would be cross, but at least the pup would be safe.

Hurrying back to her room, she set her alarm clock for five before climbing into bed. In just a few hours she would begin her rescue plan.

Bea kept dreaming of caves and seals, then waking up to check the time. When her alarm went at five o'clock, she jumped out of bed and pulled on jeans and a T-shirt. Then she took a flashlight from her drawer. There was still an hour or two till sunrise, and she would need the light to see her way along the shore.

After tiptoeing downstairs, she grabbed her raincoat and raced to the orchard. She climbed the plum tree that grew next to the palace wall, before jumping to the other side. Then she hurried down the hill into Savara.

A fierce wind swept along the seafront, and Bea shivered under her raincoat. It was strange seeing the streets so empty. The moon peeped between the storm clouds, turning the puddles on the pavement silver. The branches of the palm trees waved in the wind like the arms of angry monsters.

Bea raced down the sandy beach with the roar of the ocean filling her ears. Waves were crashing against the cliff, sending spray flying into the air. As she reached the headland, a jagged white line flashed across the distant sky, followed by a growl of thunder. Bea caught her breath. The storm was still out at sea, but it was getting closer. She shone the flashlight on the pale sand, picking her way around the rock pools.

"Snowy? Are you all right?" Bea

hurried to the mouth of the cave, her
feet slipping on the wet stones.

Another lightning flash broke from
the dark sky. Then blackness settled over
everything again.

Bea shone her flashlight into the cave and found Snowy exactly where she and Keira had left him. She crouched beside the seal pup and stroked his soft head. She wished Keira was here helping her again. Moving the creature by herself wasn't going to be easy.

Snowy yelped as thunder rolled across the bay.

"Shh! Don't worry—I'm going to look after you," Bea whispered, rubbing his furry coat.

The moon came out again, casting bright flecks across the wild sea. Bea frowned. The water was higher than it should be at low tide, and the thunder was growing louder, too. If the storm was approaching, there was no time to lose.

Bea stuck her flashlight in her pocket and laid her raincoat on the sand beside

the little seal. As she gently pushed him
onto it, Snowy began to wriggle and
squeak. Bea picked him up, all wrapped
in the raincoat, and stumbled out of
the cave mouth just as lightning flashed
through the sky once
more. This time the
thunder came faster,
and the seal hid his
face under Bea's arm.

Bea stumbled
across the beach and
around the headland,
clutching Snowy
tightly. By the time she
reached the seafront with
its row of palm trees, her
arms ached. She sank
onto the steps of the
boardwalk and laid the

seal pup on her lap. The little animal was so heavy. How was she going to get him all the way to the palace?

She rose to her feet and lifted him up once again. As she stumbled past the harbor, lightning flashed and the clouds broke open in a sudden fierce downpour. Bea spotted the *Bouncing Barnacle* bobbing in the harbor. Maybe she could shelter in the royal boat for a while?

She crossed the gangplank slowly, careful not to lose her balance on the slippery walkway. Then she tried the cabin door, sighing with relief when she found it was unlocked. She laid Snowy gently across the cabin seat. Then she slammed the door, shutting out the growling storm.

Chapter Six

A Chance
for Snowy

The storm swirled around the harbor,
rocking the boats moored to the
quayside. Bea held on to the window
ledge as the HMS *Bouncing Barnacle*
lurched from side to side. She watched
the waves curl over like huge white
claws and smash into the harbor wall.
The rain beat faster against the roof of
the little cabin.

Bea took a deep breath. She couldn't

remember a storm as bad as this one, but she and the seal pup were tucked away safely. Surely the harbor walls would keep out the worst of the wind and the waves?

Lightning flashed right overhead, followed by a gigantic boom of thunder. Bea looked at Snowy in alarm, but the pup had closed his eyes. The storm marched in from the sea and each time lightning flashed, the harbor lit up for a few seconds. Bea caught her breath as a loose fishing net blew past and disappeared into the rainy darkness.

At last the storm slowed to a gentle patter of raindrops. The angry black clouds blew past, giving way to dull gray ones, and the roar of the wind faded. A tiny glimmer of dawn peeped between the clouds, but the seal pup still didn't open his eyes. Bea waited until the boat stopped rocking so fiercely. Then she opened the cabin door quietly, careful not to wake the baby seal.

Water glistened on the deck of the boat, and the quayside was covered with puddles. Bea spotted a small figure with a dark ponytail running past the harbor. "Keira!" she shouted. "Over here!"

Keira spun around and Bea waved wildly. "It's all right," she called as Keira came closer. "I've got Snowy here—he's safe."

Keira hurried across the gangplank. "What happened?" she panted, her eyes widening as she saw the seal pup lying on the cabin seat.

Bea explained that the caves usually flooded when there was a storm. "So I had to move him ... but I didn't get very far. He's so heavy!"

She stroked Snowy's furry head. The seal pup opened his eyes and watched the girls quietly.

"The storm was awful!" Keira crouched down next to Bea and Snowy. "Did you see all that lightning?"

"It was quite scary when the thunder got louder," Bea admitted.

"You're really brave being here all alone in the storm," said Keira. "No wonder Snowy is so quiet. It must have scared him."

Bea frowned worriedly. Snowy was lying very still and his eyes looked dull. "It's more than that," she said at last. "I think he's getting weaker. Look how he hardly lifts his head anymore."

Keira gently rubbed the seal's coat. "There must be something we can do to help. Maybe he's cold. We could wrap him up in blankets . . ."

Bea shook her head. "I don't think that'll help." Sitting down beside him, she drew the seal pup onto her lap. His head flopped, and his flippers hung loosely by his side. Bea tried stroking his cheek, but Snowy just closed his eyes again.

The next burst of lightning was just a distant flicker. Then a faint rumble of thunder like a giant's snore came from farther inland.

"At least the storm has passed now," said Keira. "Shall I hold him for a minute?"

Bea carefully passed the seal to Keira before pacing up and down the little cabin. "I think Snowy needs to be back where he belongs with the other seals. He needs his mom to look after him."

"But we don't even know where he comes from," said Keira.

"Nala Island has more seals than anywhere else I know, and it's close by, too. I'm sure Snowy must have come from there." Bea went to the little cabin window and stared at the frothy gray ocean.

The waves outside the harbor were whipped up high by the wind, but they weren't crashing against the seawall as fiercely as before. Tiny glints of daylight were peeping through the gray clouds.

"How are we supposed to get Snowy to Nala Island?" Keira stared at her friend. "Bea, you're not going to do something wild, are you?"

"We have to find a way to get there," Bea said firmly. "If we don't get Snowy back to his mom soon, it could be too late." A lump rose in her throat, and she swallowed it quickly.

Keira gazed at the seal pup. "You're

right! But we can't take the boat out on our own."

Bea bit her lip, trying hard to think. Then she noticed a light in the cabin of one of the boats nearby. "We're not the only ones here! Maybe we can get someone to help us." She dashed onto the deck, then nearly slipped on the gangplank as she rushed over to the other boat. "Excuse me! Can you help us?"

Douglas opened the cabin door and looked at Bea in surprise.

"What are you doing here, Princess Bea? Shouldn't you be safe and sound at the palace?"

Bea quickly explained about the seal pup and how she'd moved him out of the cave. "Now we've got to get him back to Nala Island. He's getting so weak."

"I see!" Douglas scratched his beard.

"So I need someone to take us there, and you've driven the *Bouncing Barnacle* loads of times," Bea went on hopefully. "You will help us, won't you?"

The fisherman frowned thoughtfully. "I know a good route to Nala Island. I can have you there and back before you blink!" He smiled. "Now let me take a look at this little seal."

Bea took him back to the royal boat. Douglas found the keys and started the ignition. The engine roared. Bea went to the cupboard and found life jackets for them all.

Keira struggled into her life jacket. "Snowy, wake up!" She crouched beside the seal pup. "I think he's getting weaker."

Bea could see the animal's tummy moving as he breathed, but his eyes stayed shut. "Poor Snowy! We'd better hurry."

Rushing down the gangplank, she undid the rope on the quayside. Then Keira helped her pull in the wooden gangway and lay it on the deck.

"Are you ready?" asked Douglas. "The sea will feel quite rough."

"We're ready!" Bea said firmly.

Douglas maneuvered the boat forward, heading for the narrow gap in the harbor wall. The *Bouncing Barnacle* rocked uneasily and then,

suddenly, they were through the harbor
entrance and out on the open sea.

Chapter Seven

Storm Waves

The *Bouncing Barnacle* dipped and lurched. Waves slapped against the sides of the boat, sending torrents of spray into the air. Bea gripped the table, trying to keep her balance. Keira gave a shriek as the boat rocked sharply again, tipping her onto the cabin floor.

"Are you all right?" Bea called.

"I'm fine!" gasped Keira. "I just feel a little seasick."

"Don't worry—I'll look after Snowy."
Bea knelt down and wrapped her arms
around the seal pup.

As they sailed on, the sky lightened
and the sea grew calmer. Bea peered
into the distance. Shouldn't they be able
to see the island's rocky outline by now?
It was hard to tell where the gray sky
ended and the gray sea began. The lights
of Savara had faded behind them, and
the jagged waves seemed to stretch on
forever.

"How long till we reach the island?"
she asked Douglas.

"We'll be there soon. It's taken a little
longer because the wind is so strong,"
the fisherman replied. "How is your seal
pup?"

"I think he's getting weaker." Bea
stroked Snowy softly and stared through

the window, hoping to see Nala Island.
She thought she saw a rocky cliff, but it
turned out to be a patch of dark cloud.

Suddenly she remembered the binoculars in the cupboard. "I know something that might help us." Bea hugged Snowy tightly before gently setting him down on the seat. Moving to the cupboard, she took the binoculars from a hook inside the door. Then she hurried to the prow of the boat and lifted them to her eyes.

Nala Island appeared in the distance, almost hidden by grayish mist. Bea's stomach swooped with excitement as the island grew bigger through the glasses. "It's all right—I can see it now! It's right there."

She went back to the cabin and passed the binoculars to Douglas. The old fisherman peered through them, before steering left a little and pushing the lever to increase the speed. The boat sprang forward, riding the highs and lows of the waves. Sea spray flew high into the air, hitting the cabin roof and trickling down the window.

Little by little the island became clearer. Its rough cliffs, dotted with grass and pink sea thrift, jutted out against the gloomy sky. Bea spotted the gray seals with their tiny white pups lying on the pale sand. The air was filled with barking seal calls and the cries of the seabirds nesting among the rocks.

Douglas pulled the lever back to slow the boat down. Then he switched off the engine a short way from the beach and lowered the anchor, just as Bea's dad had done the day before. The seal pup lifted his head and gave a faint whine.

"I think he can hear the other seals," said Keira.

Bea smiled. "That's right, Snowy. You're nearly home."

"But how do we get him to the beach?" asked Keira. "The sea looks really rough, and I don't even have a bathing suit."

"We can use the inflatable dinghy." Bea rushed out onto the deck and pulled the toggle to inflate the little orange boat. Together she and Keira carried the seal pup over and laid him in the bottom of the inflatable.

Douglas helped Bea to use the rope pulley to lower Keira and the seal pup onto the water. Then Bea climbed down the ladder into the boat.

"See you soon, girls. Good luck!" said Douglas.

The girls waved at him before
taking the oars and starting to paddle.
The wind whistled around the island,
whipping the waves up high.

"It doesn't feel like we're getting any
closer!" Keira called over the whoosh of
the waves.

Bea glanced at the shore. They had
rowed for a while, but the beach still
seemed a long way away. "We have to
keep going! It's sure to get easier, right?"

A tall wave slapped the inflatable,
filling the bottom with water. The seal
pup gave a tiny yelp. Bea scooped the
water out as best she could and dug her
paddle into the sea again. What if the
rough waves tipped the inflatable over?
She and Keira had life jackets, but the
seal pup might be too weak to swim.

At last the waves grew calmer as they

came closer to the shore. The current pushed them toward a row of dark rocks at the end of the beach. Bea jumped from the boat and waded through the warm water, pulling the inflatable toward the shore.

Keira jumped out, too, and helped to hold the boat steady. "Don't you think we should land closer to the other seals?"

"No, we might scare them," said Bea. "My dad says you should always keep away from mother seals and their babies so you don't disturb them."

The bottom of the inflatable bumped against the sand, and Bea started hauling it out of the shallows.

"Bea, wait!" Keira wiped the sea spray out of her eyes. "If we don't get closer, how will Snowy ever find his mom? He's much too weak to get across the beach by himself."

Bea looked at the exhausted seal pup lying in the orange dinghy. She knew Keira was right. The beach stretched a long way, and Snowy's mother would never hear him over the barking of the other seals unless he was closer. "It's just that the inflatable is so big and bright . . . Maybe we can sneak him closer by lifting him out of the boat and carrying him through the water."

The girls took off their life jackets and left them inside the inflatable, which they pulled up onto the sand beside the rocks. Then they lifted Snowy back into the shallows, holding him carefully under his tummy. The seal pup seemed to enjoy the water, swishing his flippers weakly.

"It's all right, Snowy! We're almost there now." Bea stroked his white fur, and excitement fizzed inside her. Soon Snowy would be back with the other seals again. She hoped with all her heart that his mother would be there to meet him!

Chapter Eight
Snowy Comes Home

Bea and Keira waded through the sea, as Bea held Snowy tightly to her chest. The water came up to their waists, and now and then a wave slapped against them.

The seal pup dipped his nose in the water and gave a soft yelp. Bea kept a determined grip on the little animal. Farther along, the sand was full of grown-up seals and fluffy white pups. If

they could get Snowy closer, he might
be able find his mother again.

Gradually, the sea became shallower.
"We should move really slowly," whispered
Bea, "so that we don't scare the seals."

They waded forward slowly, trying to
stay quiet, until Keira suddenly fell over
with a huge splash.

"Are you all right?" cried Bea.

"I'm fine! I just tripped over a rock under the water." Keira winced as she got up. "I think I scraped my knee."

"We've got some Band-Aids back on the *Bouncing Barnacle*. As soon as we get back, I'll find one for you." Bea struggled to hold on to Snowy as an extra-large wave crashed into them.

"I'll be okay. It doesn't hurt that much," Keira said bravely, but she limped when she tried to walk.

"You should wait here," Bea said. "I can take him. It's not much farther."

"Thanks, Bea!" Keira kissed Snowy's fur. "Goodbye, Snowy! I'll never forget you."

Bea kept on wading through the shallow water, holding Snowy tightly. The beach was full of large gray seals with their pups, and as she drew closer, the noise became deafening. At last, Bea stepped onto the sand. The seals close by looked at her in alarm.

Bea crept farther up the beach and laid Snowy gently on the sand, then grabbed her coat and darted behind some large rocks. She watched anxiously. What if Snowy's mother didn't hear him? What if she was out at sea hunting for fish?

The seal pups on the beach called for their mothers with long, squeaky cries, but Snowy stayed quiet.

"Come on, Snowy!" whispered Bea. "You have to call out like the others."

At first Snowy didn't move. Then, at last, he lifted his head and gave a soft cry.

Bea peeked around the seaweed-

covered rocks. If only Snowy would call louder like the other seal pups!

Snowy lifted his head again and gave a louder yelp. Then he gave two more cries before dropping his head on the sand in exhaustion.

Bea held her breath. Then, from farther up the beach came an answering bark.

A large gray seal pulled herself across the sand, barking loudly. Snowy's whiskers quivered and he gave another cry. The mother seal stopped, turning her head from side to side as she listened for the sound. Then she rushed up to Snowy and sniffed his snow-white fur.

Bea smiled widely as Snowy and his mom touched noses. She turned around to make a big thumbs-up signal to Keira, who grinned and waved back.

Snowy yelped once more, and his mother gave an answering bark. Then the seal pup cuddled against his mother's side and closed his eyes. Bea's heart rose as she watched them settle down together on the sand. At last she tiptoed back into the shallows to meet Keira.

"You were right, Bea!" Keira beamed. "This was exactly the right place to bring Snowy."

"I'm really glad you were here with

me." Bea took Keira's arm and helped her limp back to the inflatable.

The girls put on their life jackets and rowed back to the *Bouncing Barnacle*. The storm winds had quieted into a cheerful breeze, and patches of blue sky peeped between the clouds. Bea grabbed the binoculars as soon as she was back on deck. She could just about make out the shape of Snowy and his mom still cuddled up on the sand.

Bea and Keira put away the inflatable dinghy while Douglas switched on the boat's engine. Then they lifted the anchor and the fisherman swung the wheel around, steering them back toward Savara.

The journey back was much quicker, and as they sailed into the harbor, the sun came out from behind the clouds. The quayside was empty except for a small flock of seagulls sitting on the harbor wall.

Bea smiled as Douglas gave back the keys to the *Bouncing Barnacle.* "Thank you for helping us. We really couldn't have done it without you!" She hesitated. "My dad doesn't exactly know about the seal, and . . ."

"That's all right," said the fisherman. "I'll let you tell him when you're ready."

Bea nodded with relief. She remembered how much her dad had wanted to protect the island's seals from noisy boats. Sometimes he showed that he really was an animal lover after all. "I will explain it all to him one day," she told Douglas, "and I think he'll be happy that we saved Snowy."

Douglas nodded and gave her a crinkly-eyed smile.

The church clock chimed seven. The row of seagulls flapped into the air and flew off over the waves.

"I didn't realize it was still so early," said Keira. "It feels like we've been sailing for hours, but it's not even breakfast time yet."

"I wish it was! I'm really hungry." Bea's stomach rumbled as she slid the gangplank into place.

"Maybe you could come to the Sleepy Gull Café for breakfast," suggested Keira. "There'll be sausages and hash browns, and lots of chocolate milk."

"Mmm, that sounds good." Bea closed the cabin door.

The girls waved goodbye to Douglas and made their way along the harbor. They linked arms as they headed up the hill toward the Sleepy Gull Café.

Stopping at the top of the cliff, they gazed across the sea to Nala Island—now just a tiny dot in the distance.

"I really hope we meet Snowy again one day," said Keira.

"Me too!" Bea opened the café door and breathed in the delicious cooking smells inside. "Come on—I could eat a mountain!"

Chapter Nine

Fun in the Waves

"Bea, where are you going with that picnic basket?" Natasha called across Savara Beach. "Come back! You're going to get the food wet."

Bea ran down to the water's edge and gazed out to sea. It had been three weeks since she and Keira had taken Snowy across to Nala Island to find his mother, and Bea had thought about the seal pup every day. Had he grown a lot bigger since then? Maybe he had even learned to swim! She kept hoping for a chance to see him, but her father had been too busy to sail the *Bouncing Barnacle* over to the island.

"Bea, don't run off with the chocolate-chip muffins," yelled Alfie.

Bea turned back, grinning. "Don't worry, I've only had three. Just kidding!" She let go as Alfie wrestled the basket from her hands.

"Alfie, don't be silly!" called Natasha. "What will people say if they see you behaving like that? I knew this picnic was a bad idea."

"At least it's a sunny day, Princess Natasha," said Nancy, who was following them with the picnic blanket under her arm. "It's nice to see the sunshine after all the windy weather."

Bea spotted Keira coming down the cliff path. She ran to meet her friend while Natasha and Nancy spread out the picnic blanket and Alfie stood guard over the basket of food. Keira had brought parcels of spring rolls and delicious pizza

slices from the Sleepy Gull Café, and soon they were all settled on the blanket with cups of lemonade and plates full of food.

Alfie jumped up first, his mouth full of chocolate-chip muffin. "I'm going to build a sand fort with a moat."

"I'll help you, Prince Alfie." Nancy picked up a bucket and shovel.

"Can we go around the corner to Silver Rock Bay?" Bea asked the maid. "The rock pools are so much better there."

"All right, Princess Bea," said Nancy. "Be sensible, won't you?"

Keira and Bea grabbed fishing nets and buckets and raced around the headland into Silver Rock Bay. Bea ran straight to the place where they'd found the seal three weeks ago. She gazed at the little rock pool where the pup had first splashed and sighed deeply. "The place seems so empty without Snowy."

"I know!" said Keira. "I just wish we could see him one more time."

"At least we know he's happy now." Bea managed a smile. "Shall we see who can catch the most crabs?"

They fished in the rock pools for a while, catching tiny crabs and silvery fish and counting them before putting them back again. Then they took off their pants and shirts and ran into the sea in their swimsuits. The sun beamed down, and the waves crashed onto the sand in a rush of white sea-foam.

"Wahoo!" yelled Bea, jumping over one breaker after another.

Keira threw herself into the sea with a huge splash, splattering water all over Bea. Then they swam around in the shallows, letting each new wave take them for a ride.

"I suppose we should go back," Keira said at last. "We've been here for ages."

"Let's stay a few more minutes." Bea floated around on her back, her dark hair waving in the water like a sea anemone. "The sea is so warm today. It makes me wish I could live here forever like a seal!"

There was a squeaky bark close to her ear. Bea was so surprised that she lost her balance. Dipping below the surface, she came up spluttering. "What was that? Did you hear something?"

"Hear what?" Keira frowned. "Are you all right, Bea?"

"I'm sure I heard something . . ." Bea stared thoughtfully at the waves.

A moment later, a silky gray head popped up from below the surface. Two large black eyes watched her curiously, and the seal twitched his dark whiskers before diving back below the water again. Then two more seal faces popped up a short distance away.

"Seals!" cried Keira. "They must be here looking for fish."

Bea spotted a smaller seal with patches of white fur across his gray coat. "Look, Keira! Do you think that's Snowy?"

Keira's face lit up. "It might be! He still has a few patches of baby fur."

"Snowy!" Bea called softly. "Is that you?"

The little seal dipped below the water, appearing in a different spot a second later. Then he swam right up to Bea and brushed against her. Bea stroked his silky coat, laughing as Snowy popped his nose out of the sea and shook the water off his whiskers.

"Snowy, you came back to see us!" cried Keira.

The seal barked softly and glided all around them, flicking his tail. Bea dived into the water and swam with the pup. Keira joined in, too, and they floated and dived and flicked water over each other.

Bea stopped to catch her breath. "You're such a good swimmer, Snowy!"

"I bet seals learn to swim really quickly," said Keira admiringly. "Look how graceful he is!"

The little seal popped up right beside Bea and Keira and gave a happy bark. Bea laughed and touched noses with him. Then the girls dived in and swam some more. Snowy zoomed all around, swishing his tail.

"Princess Bea! Keira! Time to go," Nancy called from the beach.

"Just five more minutes!" cried Bea.

"I'm afraid we have to go now," said Nancy. "Come on, girls!"

Bea touched noses with Snowy one more time. "Goodbye, Snowy! I hope you catch lots of fish. We promise to come back and see you again soon!"

The girls waded back to the shore and picked up their fishing nets. Bea turned around to wave as they left the bay and saw one last glimpse of a silky tail flicking above the water.

"Snowy looks really healthy and strong," said Keira. "I'm so happy we rescued him."

Bea smiled. "Me too! Helping animals is the best thing in the whole world."

Thank you for reading this **Feiwel and Friends** book.

The Friends who made

ROYAL RESCUES
The Cuddly Seal

possible are:

Jean Feiwel, Publisher

Liz Szabla, Associate Publisher

Rich Deas, Senior Creative Director

Holly West, Senior Editor

Anna Roberto, Senior Editor

Kat Brzozowski, Senior Editor

Kim Waymer, Senior Production Manager

Dawn Ryan, Senior Managing Editor

Foyinsi Adegbonmire, Editorial Assistant

Emily Settle, Associate Editor

Rachel Diebel, Assistant Editor

Cindy De la Cruz, Associate Designer

Ilana Worrell, Senior Production Editor

Follow us on Facebook or visit us online at mackids.com

OUR BOOKS ARE FRIENDS FOR LIFE